RANGO

THE NEW SHERIFF IN TOWN

By
ANNIE AUERBACH

Based on the screenplay written by
JOHN LOGAN

Story by
JOHN LOGAN, GORE VERBINSKI, *and* **JAMES WARD BYRKIT**

STERLING

New York / London
www.sterlingpublishing.com/kids

WHOOSH! A tidal wave of water pushed Rango, a pet chameleon who was lost in the desert, right out of the drainpipe where he was sleeping. Blinking his eyes sleepily at the blazing hot sun, Rango awoke—to find himself face-to-face with a cowboy boot. It belonged to a lizard named Beans.

"You're not from around here, are you?" Beans asked suspiciously. "Who are you?"

"Who am I?" repeated Rango. He was tired, confused, and thirsty.

"I'm asking the questions here!" Beans snapped and climbed into her wagon. "So, are you gonna die out here, or do you want a ride into town?"

"No . . . I mean, yes, please!" Rango said. He was happy to get back to civilization, even if civilization was a small town called Dirt.

Even though Dirt was small, it was full of interesting characters.

Rango tried to copy the cowboys' swagger and strutted into the local saloon. Right away, the music stopped. Everyone stared at Rango, including a bullfrog named Buford who was behind the counter. Rango told a story that made him seem like a big shot.

"I'd like a glass of water," Rango said to Buford.

Everyone laughed. There wasn't enough water in Dirt. Everyone had to drink cactus juice instead.

Suddenly, the saloon doors flew open. In walked a mean Gila monster named Bad Bill, Chorizo the rat, and two twitchy rabbits named Stump and Kinski.

The townsfolk didn't like strangers, but Bad Bill liked them least of all. He challenged Rango to a showdown.

Rango gulped. He knew he was in trouble.

Outside, Rango and Bad Bill took their positions on either end of Main Street. Rango's legs rattled in his boots.

A fierce red-tailed hawk quietly landed behind him. Rango had no idea the hawk was there. But Bad Bill saw it—and ran off!

"That's what I'm talking about!" Rango announced proudly. "Things are going to be different around here now that Rango's in town."

Finally, Rango turned around and saw the hawk. He ran for his life!

The hungry hawk chased Rango all around town until a water tower accidentally fell on top of him.

All the townsfolk thought Rango was a hero!

The mayor of Dirt wanted to meet Rango. The mayor was an old turtle in a wheelchair. His office overlooked the entire town.

"It's a hard life here," the mayor told him as they peered out at the dry, dusty street. "People have to believe in something, and right now they believe in you."

The mayor opened a leather box and picked out a sheriff star. He told Rango, "I think there's a future for this town, and I hope you'll be part of it."

Rango smiled and picked up the star. He was the new sheriff of Dirt.

The next morning, Sheriff Rango heard terrible news. The bank had been robbed! Someone had dug a hole right through the middle of the vault floor and stolen all the water the town had saved. In Dirt, the townsfolk treated water like money.

Rango had no idea what to do.

The mayor suggested Rango form a posse to find the robbers. So Rango did.

"Now, we ride!" Rango shouted, and the posse took off, racing across the desert on the backs of roadrunners.

There was just one problem: Rango didn't know where he was going. He returned to the scene of the crime and made Wounded Bird his deputy.

"You'll be in charge of all tracking and finding of villains," Rango told him. "So which way do you think they went?"

Wounded Bird pointed to the big hole in the street.

Rango was impressed.

"Oh . . . you're good," he said.

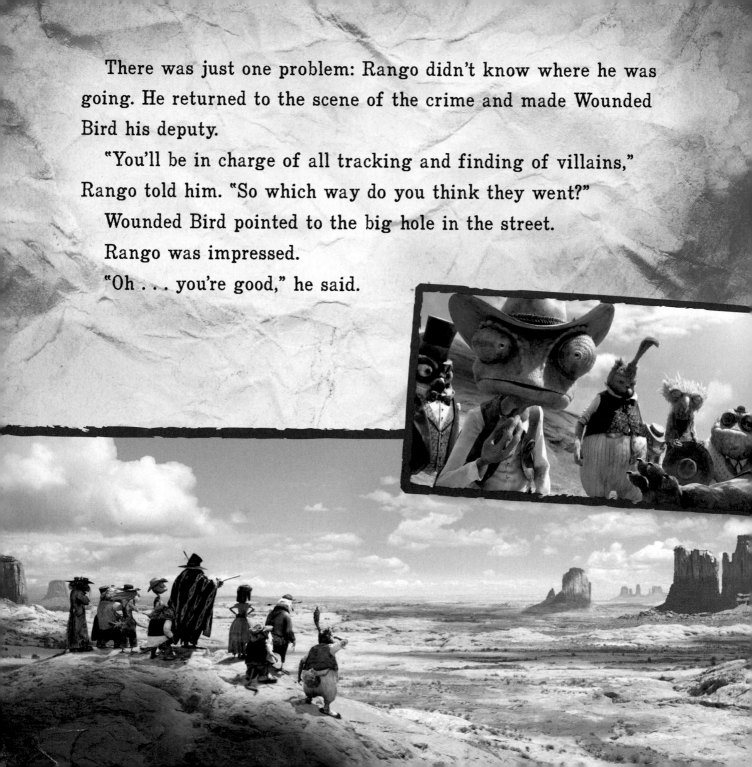

Miss Beans, Rango, and the rest of the posse crawled down into the hole and journeyed through underground tunnels. They ended up in a prairie dog town. Rango spotted one of the prairie dogs pulling a wagon with a big bottle inside.

"It's the water!" exclaimed Rango.

The posse surrounded the prairie dogs.

"Get your hands up where we can see 'em," Rango ordered.
"You and your kin are under arrest for bank robbery."

Jedidiah, one of the prairie dogs, shook his head. "Sheriff, we
tunneled into that vault, but there was nothing in it. Somebody
robbed the bank *before* we robbed it."

Another one of the prairie dogs, Ezekiel, explained that he found the empty bottle in the desert. Rango and the posse looked for themselves. It was true! The bottle was empty!

Everyone was puzzled. Rango vowed to solve the mystery of the missing water. He wanted to be a real hero.

Back in Dirt, Rango tried to cheer up a rodent named Spoons and the rest of the townsfolk. He almost succeeded . . . until Rattlesnake Jake slithered in.

Rattlesnake Jake had wicked, black eyes, a black cowboy hat, and a deadly tail. He had heard about Dirt's new sheriff.

"You're a fake and coward," Jake hissed and coiled his body around Rango.

Stuck inside the snake's grip, Rango had no choice. He admitted he had lied when he first got to town. He wasn't a big shot after all.

Rattlesnake Jake ordered Rango out of town.

Rango walked out of Dirt and into the desert. He was ashamed that he had let everyone down.

Then he saw something strange: A cactus was moving across the sand looking for water! Beans had told him a similar story, but she said it was only a legend.

"They follow the water!" Rango exclaimed and went after the cactus.

Rango ran to the top of a hill. He couldn't believe his eyes. There lay a giant water pipe with an emergency shut-off switch.

Rango thought back to his time in Dirt. Rango knew it was his destiny to save it!

"No man can walk out on his own story," he said. "I'm going back!"

Back in town, Rango challenged Rattlesnake Jake to a showdown on Main Street.

BONG! When the clock struck high noon, they both moved slowly toward one another. Rango's eyes narrowed, and he ate a bug.

When Jake was standing right over a patched-up hole on the dirt road, Rango said one word: "Thirsty?"

WHOOSH! Water exploded out of the hole and sent Jake spinning into the air. When Jake landed, he found himself face-to-face with the mayor.

The old turtle had been controlling the water supply the whole time. He had turned off the water and tried to run everyone out of town.

Rattlesnake Jake dragged the mayor away.

"Rango! You brought the water back, just like you promised!" said Priscilla.

The townsfolk whooped and hollered. There were tidal waves of water everywhere.

Rango smiled and nodded. "Well, I don't know about you all, but I could sure go for a swim!"

There was so much water that the townsfolk decided to change the name of the town from Dirt to Mud!

Would the future hold more challenges for our hero? Definitely. Would he triumph again? Possibly—but if nothing else, brave Rango would be at the ready, fighting for truth, justice, and the desert way!

★ BEHIND THE SCENES ★

The amazing art and life-like animation for *Rango* was not made overnight. It took artists and illustrators months to perfect every last detail of the characters. Before making it to the big screen, the talented team at Industrial Light and Magic created hundreds of character and set sketches, sculptures, and paintings for inspiration and research. Their animation experts then took that hand-drawn artwork and used it as a basis for the final CGI (computer-generated imagery) animation you see in theaters. Here is some "behind-the-scenes" art that shows how *Rango* came to life.

Sketch of the saloon

Final version of the saloon

Painting of Beans and Priscilla

Drawing of Rango

Painting of the fallen water tower

Painting of the flooded bank